The Brave Little Tailor

a retelling of the Grimm's fairy tale

by Eric Blair

illustrated by David Shaw

PICTURE WINDOW BOOKS

a capstone imprint

My First Classic Story is published by Picture Window Books
A Capstone Imprint
151 Good Counsel Drive, P.O. Box 669
Mankato, Minnesota 56002
www.capstonepub.com

Library of Congress Cataloging-in-Publication data
Blair, Eric.
The brave little tailor : a retelling of the Grimms' fairy tale
retold by Eric Blair ; illustrated by David Shaw.
p. cm. — (My first classic story)
Summary: An easy-to-read retelling of the classic
tale of a tailor whose boast about killing seven flies
at one blow leads him to even greater feats.
ISBN 978-1-4048-6074-2 (library binding)
[1. Fairy tales. 2. Folklore—Germany.] I. Shaw, David, 1947- ill.
II. Grimm, Jacob, 1785-1863. III. Grimm, Wilhelm, 1786-1859.
IV. Brave little tailor. English. V. Title.
PZ8.B5688Br 2011
398.2—dc22
[E]   2010003622

Art Director: Kay Fraser
Graphic Designer: Emily Harris

The story of *The Brave Little Tailor* has been passed down for generations. There are many versions of the story. The following tale is a retelling of the original version. While the story has been cut for length and level, the basic elements of the classic tale remain.

One day, seven flies were bugging a young tailor.

With one blow, he killed all seven flies.

"I must tell everyone about this!" he said.

The tailor made a belt that read "seven at one blow." Then the little tailor packed and left.

On his trip, he met a giant. The tailor said,
"Look at my belt."

The giant thought the tailor had killed seven men with one blow. The giant was afraid. He came up with a plan.

"You can stay with me and my brothers tonight," the giant said.

The giant's bed was too big, so the tailor slept on the floor. That night, the giant crept into the room. The giant thought he had killed the tailor.

The giants were surprised when they saw
the tailor the next day.

While the tailor napped, people saw his belt.
"Seven at one blow. What a hero! We should
tell the king," they said.

The king gave the tailor a place in his army.

The other soldiers were mad. "If you don't get rid of him, we are leaving," they said.

The king had a plan. "Two mean giants live in the forest. If you kill them, you can marry my daughter and become king."

"That's easy for a man who kills seven at one blow," the tailor said.

The tailor went to the forest. He dropped stones onto the sleeping giants.

The giants didn't know what was happening.

They began to fight.

The giants tore trees from the ground and beat each other to death. The tailor went back to the king.

"Now you must catch a unicorn," the
king said.

"That's easy for a man who kills seven at one blow," the tailor said.

When the unicorn saw the tailor, he
rushed to spike him with his horn.

The tailor jumped out of the way. The unicorn's horn got stuck.

"Now you must catch a wild boar," said the king.

"That's easy for a man who kills seven at one blow," the tailor said.

The boar saw the tailor and chased him.
The tailor trapped the boar in a chapel.

The tailor went to claim his reward. The king's daughter had to marry the tailor.

One night, the tailor was talking in his sleep. "Patch those pants, lad," he said. His wife told her father the man had lied. They sent men to kill the tailor that night. The tailor found out about this plan.

That night, he pretended to talk in his sleep.
"I killed seven at one blow and two giants.
I caught a unicorn and a wild boar. Why
should I fear the men at the door?"

The men ran away, and the tailor remained
king all his life.